5 Minutes

Jimmy Knowles

To Susie and the three boys

About the Author

Jimmy Knowles was used to his mum asking how school had gone today. "But mum, you've been asking me that for 50 years!" Ok, so having started at the age of 4, he liked it all so much he never left! Schooled in Yorkshire, university in Wales, and back to school via Surrey to Devon, Jim has taught Sociology in a succession of English schools and colleges for over 30 years. Latterly, he has worked as an Examinations Officer. This book hints at his experiences and unfailing humour as he unpacks a typical examination season in a West Country Secondary School.

Foreword

Sitting in the audience at an Adam Kay theatre representation of his "This is Going to Hurt" book gave me real food for thought.

I have immensely enjoyed his books, particularly for the way in which he wraps up so many social comments about the state of the NHS in a personalised and hilarious way. I was now watching him standing on the stage, armed only with a microphone and keyboard, holding the rapt attention of a large crowd

Mmmmm wonder if I could do that...keep a diary of the daily goings on of a common examination officer?

Well, if you are in a bookshop (or even reading online) perusing this foreword and haven't read any Adam Kay stuff, go and have a look right now.... oh actually, maybe not...buy this book first, then go have a look. He seems to be doing ok for himself, so I could do with the money.

So with ideas of future royalties, a tour planned, a TV series, and appearances as a celebrity on House of Games (come on, you only ever recognise 1 or 2 people on there), here I am launching forth with a behind-the-scenes look into what goes on in a West Country Secondary school during the external exam season between May and June.

Names, situations, gender, etc., have been slightly tampered with to preserve anonymity – but let's face it - to avoid litigation!

Having been an examination officer for 10 years on the back of a 30-year teaching career I hope that the diaries herein, if not touching the macabre depths of Mr Kay's exposition, at least give you something to chuckle over and question about our education system today.

Table of Contents

Week 1

It is all very strange – after 2 years of no "official" examinations due to the well-documented situation – here we are, ready to go

Although, to be fair, there have been exams during the lockdown era – just that we have not been able to call them exams – "assessments" is the buzzword.

Students sat them like exams, answered exam-style papers under exam conditions, got them marked, and ended up with grades. The main difference was that school staff did all the work...and exam boards still charged us!

So here I am in the exam hall, which like many schools, has an alter ego of Sports Hall the rest of the year – a tin and breeze block building with no windows and overhead archaic heating designed for people running around in next to nothing instead of sitting there writing away for a few hours.

With me are my team of trusty (mainly!) invigilators whom you will meet along the journey. Chief invigilator and man responsible for organising the rest is Methuselah – an ancient grumpy sausage who should have headed to the knacker's yard eons ago but somehow manages to turn up every year to lick the rest into shape.

An ex–teacher like myself and most of the team - he 'knows the kids'. Well, in truth, he probably felt he knew them back in the 80s but has no chance now in his 70th year. He wonders why the little snowflakes aren't as robust as they once were....and boy are we in for a treat with post covid mental and behavioural fallout!

Monday

The exam hall is divided up like a great big battleship grid with columns A-K and numbers 1 – 20. In fact, there is a balcony from which I peer down at the students beavering away. As they look up reassured, little do they realise that Methuselah is texting co-ordinates from another exam room to see if he gets a hit on a ginger kid!

It's a relatively uneventful low-key start to the season with RE GCSE – Welsh board. There are 4 main exam boards...well 3 plus the Welsh!

Although in Wales, the WJEC is probably a major player - for us, they are a minor provider. Each board has its own idiosyncrasies, and the Welsh have the most complicated website and the longest subject codes in the world. I think the code generator lives in Llainfairpwllgwyngyllgogerychwyrnrobwlllantysilio gogogoch and is only working to type.

Welsh RE code C120U10-1/3

Edexcel Maths Code: 1MA

Still, they are the friendliest lot on the phone and always make me want to answer them in my best *Uncle Bryn* voice.

Tuesday

Biology this morning, and one student with an extreme blood phobia is rather worried that any question in this area may lead to him fainting, throwing up, or having a panic attack and running out. To me, the latter option is the most preferable as I don't want to have to carry him out, nor do I want to have to clean up a whole load of...you get the picture. How would we get rid of the smell? And I don't want to kick off a domino effect with 150 of them starting to retch.

Note to self – is there still a bucket somewhere with magic sand to throw down?

Wednesday

My mobile goes off in my pocket (vibration only, of course). Oh, the irony of having to carry my phone everywhere whilst depriving the teens of theirs every exam.

It is Barney McGrew in the office.

Barney is a female, but because of her surname and a longing for my childhood days of "Watch with mother" and Trumpton being my favourite, I have given her the Barney moniker. In fact, I have ascribed the firemen character names to the whole office – or Trumpton as I like to call it.

So there is Pugh, Pugh, Barney McGrew, Cuthbert, Dibble, Grub

(well, only one Pugh, and I don't want to be unkind, so there is no Grub)

Anyway, let me tell you about Trumpton, aka The Main Office...they are the real engine rooms and powerhouses of any school. My office is an all-female affair, and I often visit due to the nature of my work - but mainly to get the view from Planet Venus!

An example: My wife was going out for the day, and so I asked if I should save her some food for tea when she returned. 'No, don't worry,' she said.

So I didn't...either worry or save her any food. When she returned, she was furious!

I played this scenario through with a few male members of staff, and they were in one accord...she had stated that she didn't want anything and, therefore, my behaviour was beyond reproach.

But on Planet Venus, aka the front office, the response was, "You idiot, of course, she wanted you to save her some food...."

I like to think that I help give them insight into the Planet Mars male world...but of course, they have that well sussed.

Anyway, back to the call. She puts through Mrs Kelly, mum to Freddie in Year 11....

***

"Hi, Mr Knowles. I am afraid that Fred got soaked through on his way to the bus stop and has now returned home and doesn't really feel like it today...can he do his English tomorrow..."

"No, you silly cow – this is the culmination of years of preparation, all the way through secondary school has been mounting to this moment, drag him by the ear back to the bus stop, kick him up the bum, and in no uncertain terms get him on a bus and get him to school pronto!"

...is what I was saying in my head - but a more professional tone emerged from my mouth...

"Sorry to hear of your troubles Mrs Kelly but unfortunately, GCSE exams cannot be re-arranged, and therefore it is really best that you get him to school in time to start the exam."

***

Thursday

Blood trickling over the computer keyboard, dripping onto the chair, trailing across the floor, out of the door, down the stairs, and stopping outside the loo.

Inside is Lucy, door ajar as she stuffs paper towels up her nostrils as Katie, her friend, offers moral support.

"Nothing to worry about, Sir! I get them all the time," she chirps cheerfully through a handful of bloody towels.

Turns out that in the computer room, just in the pre-exam sort-out, Lucy's nose started gushing, and she quickly moved to sort herself out.

Nothing to worry about...nothing to worry about! Alright, for her but the crimson trail has left me rather green, and how am I going to get blood out of a keyboard?

Anyway, being the responsible adult, I helped her get sorted...well, I sit on a seat near the loo as Katie sorts her. And get her back to the exam room as soon as she feels ready. I am not such an exam ogre that I insist she gets there for the 09:00 start, but give her 10 minutes to clean up, rest up and ensure that the flow has stopped.

On return, Meth has cleaned the keyboard, desk, seat, and floor with his bright blue gloves, a big blue roll of industrial-strength paper towel, and sanitiser spray. Covid has been good for something!

Reseated elsewhere and still in a calm, jovial mood, Lucy starts her exam 15 minutes late - but will still be given the full-time allocation.

A shriek from outside the door – I pop my head out to encounter a young boy with his parents being shown around as a potential new Year 7 student.

Oops, forgot to clean up the mess outside the room, and the darkening, gel-like red marks glistening on the stairs helped me to realise that, actually, what I thought was going to be a tame tale compared with Mr Kay's hospital adventures may have some gore potential after all.

Friday

Maths GCSE plus various A Levels makes for a full house. Students amass outside the exam room and, as they enter, are programmed (via many assemblies and lower school practice exams) to flip into exam mode as soon as they come through the door. They silently walk to their seats in a sensible manner (or get kicked out and made to re-enter in a suitable fashion if any Monty Pythonesque silly walks occur).

Except today when our wonderful American Head decides to evoke her transatlantic 'pep' assembly technique on the way in whooping, high-fiving, and telling them, 'You got this.' Fortunately, the British and West Country response is one of bemusement as the students roll their eyes and give her a patronising smile as they brush past her and find their seats.

So suitably 'pepped', they are ready to tackle the non-calculator exam.

Now exam equipment is the bane of the Exams Officer – well, in truth, tis one of a number of 'banes'. We have to provide calculators, pens, pencils, rulers, etc. Of course, students are supposed to come tooled up with such implements in their transparent pencil case (or plastic bag, etc.), and most do, to be fair.

But a sizeable chunk always forgets something (or never bothered to get one in the first place). Their sense of entitlement knows no bounds; I would dearly love to tell them 'tough' you ain't got it, then you do without.

It's a catch-22 because as soon as you try that, you incur the wrath of parents, staff, the Senior

Leadership Team (SLT for short), and Uncle Tom Cobbley... and you just avoid the potential conflicts. Even trying with lower school students in mocks is deemed 'unacceptable'. "Don't want to cause anxiety issues" ...what about teaching some "responsibility issues?"

In the afternoon, we have a full-on panic attack situation as Claire rushes out of one of the satellite rooms. One of the roving invigilators literally catches her flying down the stairs and helps her to sit down on a seat outside the room. Claire slumps onto the floor as the cool tiles are refreshing. One of our wonderful counsellors Jane, comes to the rescue with sage advice and the 54321 grounding techniques. 30 mins later, Claire is back in the exam – physically if not mentally!

For students with specifically identified issues, we are allowed to issue time-out cards, so students have time frozen whilst they get themselves together. I fear Claire is a whisker away from dropping out altogether, despite all the input of student services and the counselling team.

Week 2

Monday

"2 sociologists sunbathing on the beach

"Have you read Marx?"

"Yes, I think it's these wicker chairs."

I have a stock of jokes relating to most subjects to tell in the exam hall when I run out of things to say. It helps relax them just before opening the paper in front of them.

There are a lot of blurb to get through

No Phones

No watches

Water bottles on the floor

Silence when you leave

And so on

The art is trying to work out how soon to get students into the hall. Leave it too late, and you are rushing to start on time because you don't want to have to change the settings of the timings displayed on the screens. (We use display screens hooked up to laptops) ...but get them in too early, and you end up having to vamp like a show band until the singer is ready.

So to help with my vamping, I have a few extra things to bring up, with the fun one being a subject-relevant joke.

My Marx joke raises a few titters but mostly patronising smiles as sad dad act at the front dreams of his one-man Edinburgh fringe show. The other invigilators take the side of the crowd with moans and groans and exaggerated facial contortions.

I sign off with

"I'm here all week."

To which one wag replies:

"Sadly, so are we."

"Oh, just open your papers and get on with it…"

But thank goodness for subjects like Sociology, History and Philosophy, and Ethics. In a world where people are too readily cancelled or accused of being purveyors of false information, such critical thinking is more essential than ever.

Tuesday

Bl**dy AQA, why do they require exam officers to log in to their site (after waiting for a code to be sent to their phone) to wade through various screens to find, download and print labels to put on the sacks for returning scripts. Other exam boards provide you with the labels already to peel and stick on…GET IT SORTED!

Just one of many admin frustrations. I deal with all 4 main exam boards, and each has its own procedures, stationery, admin requirements, websites, and so on.

Take the example of stationery. If students need more paper in an exam, AQA have 4-page pink booklets, OCR have 4-page white booklets, WJEC have pink booklets too (why couldn't they pick a different colour?), and Edexcel likes to use single white sheets.

So invigilators have to be on their toes in exams knowing which boards are being serviced in the number of exams happening in the hall at any one time.

As for ordering more paper from the exam boards – not easy, is it?

Edexcel are the worst here, as they only allow you to order a batch of 100 at a time. Now I am sorry, but in English Language GCSE alone, I have 160 students, the majority of them using 2/3 extra sheets. So I spent another 20 minutes of my precious time logging in, ordering 100, then logging out. Then logging back in and ordering another 100, then...you get the picture, rinse and repeat ad infinitum.

It is like they want to guard their precious cargo and hate having to part with it. Sometimes I wonder if anyone working in these organisations has ever spent any time in schools/colleges looking at the process from the user end. It's not like they are giving "owt for nowt," with GCSEs costing £50 -90 per subject and A Levels £60 -120.

We are all used to proving that we are not robots with ridiculously confusing Americanised road pictures of traffic lights, buses, and sidewalks to tick off, but now one of the exam boards is asking me to prove "my humanity."

Wednesday

And the morning starts with meltdowns all over the shop.

One refusing to go into the exam room

One refusing to leave home to come to school

One in tears during the exam

All female – now, not a gender-biased comment and not wanting to evoke the wrath of the woke brigade, but national stats are showing significant mental health issues increasing amongst females, and this is certainly being borne out on the ground under my feet and supported by the dealings of our counsellors. Worthy of further national research.

Anyway, a rest break and TLC by an invigilator gets the tearful one back on track, gentle but firm coaxing by Jane, the counsellor, gets the reluctant one into the exam, and the mum manages to change the school refuser to school attender just a little bit late but within the window of acceptable start times.

Thinking all is at peace with the world. I get a text from a 1:1 room where a little Year 7 'cherub' (cleaned up for this missive) has banged on the door and run away.

On arrival at the scene, the culprit has been identified by the rest of his RE class, who were queued up outside (should I say 'standing in line' for when the book hits the American market!).

No "I'm Spartacus" today, it seems – all fingers squarely pointing at the offender. The Head of RE tells me that she has reprimanded, placed in detention, and read the riot act to said deviant. She scares me, so I think the little guy will be quaking in his boots.

Thursday

Henry VII: Think I might build a car park in Leicester.

Richard III: Over my dead body!

Ah, History – I love the subject, and it is a real old-school-style exam paper. A thin sheet with essay titles – write 3 in 2 ½ hours.

Takes me back to my own A Levels.

Anyway, my pre-exam blurb finishes quickly, so a joke is in order. Quite a few genuine laughs – gives me heart

Computer Science GCSE in the afternoon. This is one of those exams where many finish ridiculously early. I suspect this for 2 main reasons:

1. The tech heads know the stuff and whizz through like Billy from The Beano

2. Those who struggle know they are beat and give up...not much vamping, writing rubbish for an hour ala prose style exams here.

You know it, or you don't – no halfway house.

The exam lasts 2 ½ hours, so I release some after 1 ½ to avoid a whole hour of sitting there with a glazed face. JCQ regs state that we can't let folk go until after an hour. So after numerous nudges and requests to read through their answers one more time, I set them free.

Friday

One lad is continually late to his exams, so being the caring EO (Examinations Officer), I visit with Student Services and check with the deputy HOY.

Back in the day, we used to have Heads of Year and Deputy Heads of Year – both teachers and usually one male and one female, echoing the mum/dad at school approach.

Now we have a HOY who is a teacher supported by an admin person – the Assistant Head of Year. This, of course, saves money, but to be fair, just like civil servants in government, these admins usually have the finger on the pulse whilst their 'ministers' are torn between teaching duties and pastoral stuff.

So I approach our Assistant Head of Year 11, wondering if there are deep-seated issues, mental health, domestic upheaval, self-esteem, etc., regarding the tardy student.

"No, he's just being a dick."

Smiling all the way back to the exam hall, I am gladdened by this technical assessment and resolve to give said "dick" no more extra time to finish exams he starts late.

Each set of exams have to be collected, checked off against registers 'riffled' with those arriving from word processing and other special requirement rooms, and placed in sacks labelled and dropped off in the main office – Trumpton – to be collected by Parcelforce.

Cuthbert phones me at 4:15 to say that Parcelforce haven't arrived yet and she needs to go home as her time is up. I arrange to go and sit at her desk and wait for Pat (minus the black and White cat) to arrive in his big red van.

By 5:00 pm, I decide to phone Parcel force to see what is amiss – if parcels are not collected, I need to lock them away usually until the next day. The helpful Sandra at Parcelforce central tried to raise the local depot but no response. She agrees that this is not good enough as exam packages are given priority and will raise merry hell with them and report it up the line. I thank her for her efforts, but I am now stuck with 11 large sacks. This is compounded by it now being the weekend and half term to boot!

Week 3

Half Term

So a week off and time to recharge.

Before all that, though, I have to come to school, put the 11 sacks in the car, and drive down to the local village Post Office.

I nip in to warn Eliza that I have 11 rather large packages to send off. She smiles, opens the little glass door as I retrieve the load from the car, and zaps the labels with her scanner.

The Parcelforce van will have to collect from here. As I return to school, I am met by Fred, the caretaker, who informs me that Parcelforce Pat has arrived on site and is driving around looking for the packages. I am tempted to tell him to hide for another 30 minutes before relenting and seeking him out.

Frustrated by the fact that if only he had phoned me (as mobile details are supplied to Parcelforce), he could have saved me a lot of extra work. I treat him with controlled, thinly disguised displeasure rather than full-on manic aggression. I am too nice at times!

After this escapade, the week pans out to be a nice one of rest as we celebrate Betty's diamond jubilee.

I play 2 gigs with my band Dodger to mark the occasion in local village events. The band was originally named Coffin Dodger to reflect that we are all getting on a bit in years but to avoid potentially upsetting folk and to secure more gigs. We dropped the coffin.

I play bass, and it has been a useful release valve over the years. All covers, but with some less obvious songs, it gets people dancing. We don't take ourselves too seriously but are serious about making it sound good. We play for contributions to charity as we are all in a position not to need it as an extra income – although with fuel prices increasing, I wouldn't say no to say few quid...

The gigs pass off pleasantly and with good weather, which is a relief as they were outdoor affairs. Plus, as a result of our endeavours, we get booked for a whole host of festivals across the summer – more Little Dribbling than Glastonbury, but it keeps me out of mischief.

My secondborn is moving up north, so I spend a couple of days driving up the M5 and M1 with all his stuff as he starts post-uni proper adult life.

I stay at a nice motel in the Midlands on return and start to compile a list of the famous people I have taught over the years...well, people who have famous names, if not the original folk:

Michael Caine

Jeffrey Archer

Sharon Stone

Robbie Savage

Peter Kay

Michael Douglas

Andy Cole

Yvette Fielding

To name a few….

One real famous…ish person I did teach, I can't name here but plays in a world-renowned band.

One person I can mention…never taught …but ran into him at a gig…was a really nice guy.

I was playing at a wedding near Taunton with a function band, and as I unloaded my amp and stuff… Rudy, our sound guy, excitedly screamed out, "Peter Andre is here!" Now being far from his normal fan demographic; nevertheless, I was curious to meet him.

As I turned the corner there, he was as large as life – well, realistically, he is Pete Diddly – chatting to our geriatric brass player, Eric

"I know you from somewhere," I hear Eric say as I get closer.

"It'll come to me."

Meantime, Peter smiles at me, shakes my hand, and says

"Hello, I am Peter" As if I didn't know who he was, but I appreciated the way that he didn't assume.

And begins to chat away about how he has heard good things about us, how he knows the bride and groom etc.

I ask him if he wants to get up and sing a song with us, and a light appears on Eric's face as realisation slowly dawns...or so I thought.

Peter declines the offer saying that he just isn't ready and prepared. We continue to chat away, and suddenly Eric raises his finger

"I know who you are... you are the guy who sold me my new car!"

The wonderful singer doesn't break a sweat, throws me a wink and stays in his newly created persona, and asks how Eric is liking the car.

What a lovely genuine guy, and to this day, my kids refer to him as "dad's mate Pete" whenever he appears on TV.

On the way back from my trip, I nipped into the services and parked next to a large van with "Youth

Speedway Rider...plus the name" splattered across in orange and black. Said rider appeared back from the Costa outlet with, I assume, mum and dad all decked out in matching sporty orange and black gear to match the livery on the van.

Now speedway is not my thing...went once when I was a lad, and as a friend pointed out," Speedway so exciting – you never know who is going to win until the first bend" rang so true, and I was bored and filthy by the end of the night.

However, it gladdened my heart to see this group, whom I assumed were returning from an event back to Plymouth. Presuming the sacrifice of the young lad and his parents to fund a not-so-cheap hobby/career choice – to give up time for practice and travel to such events is no light matter.

So to all the parents, guardians, friends, etc., who invest in young folk, whatever their passion, sports, music, dancing, drama, etc., you are doing a splendid thing. Finding a passion, pursuing that passion, and helping young folk to realise and release such passions despite the sacrifices – or perhaps because of the sacrifices must lead to fewer messed up young folk, less mental stress, less loneliness, and helping them "find themselves."

On return to school, I intend to seek out our D of E co-ordinator, the sports teachers, the chess club organiser, the drama and music staff, the science club lead, and so on and just say thanks.

Thanks for providing such a variety of stuff for young folk to get involved with. Thanks for giving your time. Thanks for helping to shed post-lockdown insecurities. As a dad, as a teacher, and as someone who has been on the receiving end of such work...thanks!

As I return, I received an email from the local hospital education officer (Fran). It appears that one of our GCSE students, Hayley, has been admitted with Type 1 diabetes. As Hayley is likely to miss the next week of exams, could I contact her to arrange the delivery of papers to the hospital, where Fran will supervise her taking the exam whilst propped up in her bed? I am very impressed – some things the NHS gets bang on!

Just as I am about to head up to the school to put plans in place, I receive a message from Hayley's dad. The remarkable and stoic Hayley has left the hospital and would like to carry on with exams as though nothing much has happened. I arrange with dad for Hayley to have a time-out card as she is starting the process of monitoring her levels and will need to leave the exam at times and take on some sugar to get back up to her required safe level.

Over the next few weeks, Hayley does carry on almost as though nothing major has happened in her life. A few rest breaks where she has to leave the exam hall when flagging and rest and eat Haribo as she adjusts to her new regime, but no major hassles occur, and it's a win-win for myself and the invigilators looking after her – she brings enough Haribo to share.

Of course, I don't have favourites – but if I did, Hayley would be up there as a student of the year!

Week 4

Monday

The vast majority of students take their exams seriously, take their exam conduct seriously, and don't cheat!

However, as EOs, we have to be vigilant. Of course, no phones are allowed in the exam hall, and from this year, no watches either. Water bottles have to be transparent, and any labels have to be removed after an enterprising cheat wrote stuff inside the label for one exam at a school somewhere in the UK (not here).

One of our invigilators is an ex-Police Officer and has been tasked with checking the loos for phones and hidden notes – even lifting the cistern as she reckons a phone inside a waterproof bag will survive in there. She does stop short of searching the sanitary disposal bin!

She is also adept at looking for bulges in clothing in the exam hall and checks for anything suspicious. We have heard rumours of a particular student going to the loo a lot, and therefore we research for more information.

When students need the loo, they have to be escorted - obviously, the invigilator waits outside - and timings are recorded in a file in the exam room.

Said student has a record of going to the loo a lot and, therefore, worthy of closer investigation. It turns out that a medical record of bladder issues gives a reasonable explanation, and rumours are seemingly based on jealousy. Searches of the loos show no signs of any untoward props, and all is well with the world.

Bunny, one of our mature invigilators already despairing of the clothes or lack of on 6th form females, remarks: "Well, her dress is so tight I can see her g string through the material, so heaven knows where she could hide a phone."

The ex-Police officer launches into an in-depth and vivid description of how full-body searches suggest places where phones can be hidden; poor Bunny seems shell-shocked for the rest of the session!

Tuesday

There is always the odd idiot!

Billy has turned up to the exam and is still looking through his notes and will not enter the hall. With a few minutes to lift off, I urge him to find his seat. He refuses, so I start to close the door and tell him that it will soon be too late and we aren't going to wait for him.

Reluctantly he makes his way to his seat, which, typically, is right at the back. So I whiz through my spiel and am just about to tell them to start when up pops Billy's hand.

"Can I fill my water bottle?"

"No, too late!"

An array of silent nods and smiles from the other students shows an appreciation for knocking the little irritant down a peg or two.

Later his Maths teacher filled me in with the full picture. Billy had turned up at the Maths office demanding a calculator. He tried to help himself from the shelf and was given a rollicking from the Head of the Department. After apologising, Billy was allowed to borrow a calculator, handing his phone in for insurance.

After the exam, he had gone back to retrieve his phone. Finding the office closed, he barged into his teacher's Year 7 Maths lesson.

"Oi Smithy, here's your calculator, where's my phone...and your exam was f****ing hard.

Glad to say that Smithy gave him an almighty dressing down, and Billy's future exam attendance is now hanging in the balance!

Wednesday

So what if I don't know what Armageddon means – it's hardly the end of the world!

RE today!

'Anxiety' is a hot potato in the current educational climate. It is being used too readily as a further tool of cultural capital by some parents. I overheard one student saying to another, "Just get your doctor to write a letter saying you have anxiety, and you can get special consideration."

So on one level, "anxiety" claims are very much flavour of the season, but on other levels, there are some serious issues causing real distress.

One student who has been struggling has been advised by CAMHS (Children and Adolescent Mental Health Services) to stop attending exams for her own well-being. Now my mantra has always been "they are only exams" and need to be kept in context – there are more important things in life – like life itself.

So if they suggest stopping, then I am in full support. The problem is that not taking exams can have a negative effect, too, a sense of failure, stress about retaking, and so on—such a difficult juggling act.

I saw a recent interview where a psychologist was asked about the effects of lockdowns on the mental health of school-age students. She stated that 50% of her clients had pre-existing problems exacerbated by the lockdown, but 50% were new cases caused by the whole lockdown scenario.

On a lighter note, Joan has gone too early!

Many of our invigilators are retired folk, the seasonal nature of the job making it difficult to recruit others. However, do not read 'retired' for 'past it' as they are very much on it. But we do have a trio of females, a retired scientist, a retired lecturer, and a retired businesswoman, all alpha females who compete to be top dog at times in the exam hall. They will totally deny this as they all get on very well – but they can't fool me.

I purposely do not assign a lead role and sit back to see who takes on the duties – who takes the register, who collects the phones etc., and most important of all, who gives the "You have 5 minutes left" announcement.

The JCQ are rather vague in their ICE (Instructions for Conducting Examinations) booklet about giving a 5-minute warning:

A five-minute warning to candidates before the end of the examination is permitted. However, this is at the centre's discretion. Where candidates have different finishing times, the centre must consider the impact of giving a warning

Interestingly their wording has changed in recent times as previously the 'permitted' was 'not encouraged'. A shame, really, because the rebel in me always enjoyed going against their non-encouragement. Possibly, inspectors up and down the land found stopping it a losing battle.

I do agree that when there are many exams with differing end times in the room, it can be disruptive, so a subtle approach of going to that particular group in the hall and turning ones back on the others helps focus the warning. In general, though, we have all grown up with the "5 minutes" warning and, as much as anything, want the tradition to continue. So much has changed that holding on to this little bit of the past is comforting.

And so a long-winded route back to Joan. Well, in the alpha female battle, the opportunity to give the warning is the Victor Ludorum. So the jostling of position is a sight to behold. You have to time it to be in the correct position to deliver the spiel while at the same time keeping an eye on the clock to judge when to lift off. Countdown clocks are not allowed in exams, and I have greyed out the seconds on the digital screen making it less intrusive to students. The seconds can still be seen but only when close to the screens and with keen eyesight. As mentioned above, these three maturer ladies are very much 'on it,' but keen eyesight is not a friend of the ageing process!

WHAT ABOUT JOAN? Patience, patience! Well, today, Joan had done the jockeying to get into prime position and, with a big grin, announced: "You have 5 minutes left".

Bemused faces, a few groans, students looking at each other, Bunny and Molly beaming!

"Oh no, I've gone too soon! Sorry, you have 10 minutes left".

You could almost hear the reversing beep as red-faced Joan had to backtrack. Still, students and staff alike had a good chuckle, and all was well. The Examinations Officer on the balcony catching the eye of a few students just shrugged and smiled.

Thursday

My nemesis is here this morning, sneering out of his cab as I stare him down. He takes an age to complete his paperwork before begrudgingly moving his lorry out of the way so I can get to the car park beyond.

Let's rewind a little. This delivery lorry/truck (see, not forgetting my friends across the big pond) blocks the driveway to the car park. Not his fault as the kitchen delivery door is bang smack in the middle of a narrow one-vehicle width access drive. However, most delivery drivers wave and rush to deliver and get on their way. This one, however, takes great delight in being as slow as he can, spends ages chatting to the kitchen staff, and then sits in his cab completing his paperwork for an age and a day. All the while not meeting eye contact, not offering any word of explanation or thanks, and only seems to move because he has other deliveries to make; otherwise, he would sit there all day long gloating. I am tempted to leave my car directly blocking his exit and walk off into school for a few hours.

It doesn't seem to matter if I vary my arrival times he is always there (of course, he isn't, but it just feels that way). Maybe he has installed a tracker on my vehicle and waits for me – like the truck driver in Spielberg's 'Duel'.

There was a guy who bullied me once when I was a school kid in the first form, and he was in the fifth form (Year 7 and Year 11 in new money) – by kicking me up the backside each and every step as I descended four floors at school. After each kick, I had to say thank you, or he would boot me even harder. I can still vividly recall his platform shoes and flared ends of his trousers (well, it was the 70s). Relevance? Well, this driver is reaching the second spot behind said bully in the league table of people I hope have had horrible lives!

Anyway, back to school where every day is a 'school day'…quite literally for me at the moment. I learned an important lesson today – celery cannot be eaten quietly. Apparently, my crunching could be heard in the exam hall – I must close my office door in the future.

So I am in my office sorting out more address label printing for returning exam scripts. The AQA has emailed me and asked why some labels have not been used. For some exams, I can get them in 3 bags and therefore don't need 4 labels. I can't email them back to explain this, but I need to log on (see previous palaver) and, for each exam, fill in comments as to why I didn't need a label. After about the 20th exam, my comments get a little less charitable - "This is a waste of my time," "Better things to do," "Are you working from home making up things to occupy yourself?"

So it serves me right when for the next big exam, I have only been sent one label. I retaliate by finding the biggest sack I can and shoving them all in that. Sometimes the inner child bursts through!

A tale as old as time! Boy meets girl....Boy meets girl 2....Girl 1 finds out....Girl 1 and Girl 2 are in a fisticuffs scenario....

I discovered all this when the Assistant Head of Year 11 came to explain that at the end of the exam (where all 3 are present), I can let the row with girl 2 out first so she can chaperone her away from the temptation to brawl. I am happy to oblige, and steamy smouldering resentment and the potential for a crowd gathering around shouting "fight, fight" is averted.

Separating fighting females has always been more tricky for a teacher, in my experience. Males tend to fight in some kind of accepted rules and often are relieved to have someone break it up. Apart from the obvious issue for a male teacher trying to separate warring females, no such pseudo-

Queensberry rules exist. As such, it is very difficult to assert reasonable behaviour in the heat of the moment!

Friday

> *I have an eye of a tiger, a heart of a lion, and....*
> *a lifetime ban from Paignton Zoo!*

Biology A Level

The school backs onto a railway line – a nice steam line where the trains whistle as they pass. It's like being on Sodor! My desire is for the whistle to blow just as I tell them to stop writing. It has only happened once in the 6 Years I have been doing this job.

Today there is a rumbling outside the exam hall. A train has stopped at the signal just outside. Usually, this is momentary as the train quickly moves off, hissing as the steam picks up.

But the rumbling goes on for 10 minutes, so I take a look outside.

It is a diesel engine and has been idling there for ages. Unlike the steam engines, this old thing is grumbling away and vibrating through the walls.

Meth pops out and can hardly contain his excitement as he points out that it is a class 37 diesel engine and goes off on a long explanation about them. I smile in return but have stopped listening eons ago.

Meth is a train nerd and regularly helps out at another steam railway at weekends. I catch a little more of his diatribe and discover that its nickname is the "growler" - very apt, I just wish it would move on and growl somewhere else. I leave him to it as he moves closer to the fence to take snaps on his phone.

I nip into Trumpton for a daily dose of Heardle. When we get a few quiet minutes, we try the Heardle for the day – for the uninitiated, it is musical wordle – sort of. Basically, it is guessing the intro. Most of the fire crew are youngsters (well, compared with me), so they are usually good at the 80s or current stuff as they have young kids. Dibble is particularly good across the board, but today is my turn to shine as I know the tune and band within the first 2 seconds, Blue Oyster Cult: Don't Fear the Reaper.

Moans of "oh, I know the song," or I know it is "Don't Fear the Reaper, but I don't know the band," I leave them basking in the glory of being officially crowned "maestro"!

Week 5

Monday

So many students need coloured paper these days to help with dyslexia and other conditions. The trouble is that the exam boards align with Henry Ford and say that you can have any colour as long as it is .... white! OK, so I took a liberty there, but you get the drift.

So we have a smorgasbord of colour requests, yellow, light blue.

Dark blue, grass green, lilac, or is it violet, dark purple? So we have to photocopy the exam papers onto coloured paper every session. But we can only open papers from their sealed packs an hour before the exam, so a lot of rushing around. We have to have "2 pairs of eyes" observing the opening of the packs and sign a prepared sheet. I religiously open the papers in front of Meth each and every exam.

Can't help singing Joseph's coat song as we go..." it was red and yellow and green and brown and ochre and peach and ruby and..."

Probably have done it already Mr Osman, but it would make a good Pointless question - name a colour from Rice/Lloyd Weber Joseph song.

And whilst on the subject Mr Rice, if you ever read this, what is going on with the...

Greatest man since Noah
Only goes to show...a

Couldn't find a rhyme, got fed up, late at night, too many lemonades?

Have played in the band for the show many times...and love it!

Tuesday

Most of my jokes – well, they aren't mine – but that is the nature of jokes as they get passed around by word of mouth and the internet but my Computer Science one has a definite origin – Milton Jones

So I hope that he gives me permission to replicate it here, and if he doesn't, I hope that he will forgive me for telling it to the exam masses.

Go and see him live, he is very funny.

If you google lost servant boy –

it says that this Paige cannot be found.

Have to give a ticking-off to an invigilator today. It's a difficult one and not something I enjoy at all. Now my team are absolutely brilliant – not all are spot on at everything, but all shine in certain areas, and I have learned how to use them, where to use them...and where not to use them.

Some are great with tech and don't get phased with computers, others I can't let near the things, some seem to have number dyslexia and can't be trusted to put scripts in candidate number order, some are brilliant in one-to-one sensitive student scenarios, some are great at scribing and so on.

Molly is a no-nonsense straight, talking, totally reliable invigilator who I inherited with the role and has been doing this for 20-plus years. Her attitude at times is rather unwoke, and feels that today's students are too pampered. The trouble is she doesn't suffer fools and is short on tact.

The head has an assistant, "Big John," labelled with similar irony to Robin Hood's right-hand man in that he is a little guy. He is also rather "Type A" personality-wise, which causes some conflicts with people at times. Very organised, very into the process and not the best people person. I get on well with him, and with my more Type B personality, I appreciate someone so well organised, but I do see the problems at times.

Anyway, back to the need for a telling-off. A member of SLT came to me and asked if "I could have a word". Apparently, Molly was heard to describe Big John as a "knob".

This made me burst into laughter as I haven't heard anyone called that since my own school days. Seeing that the Assistant Head wasn't as amused, I sobered and asked where this had occurred, apparently in the main corridor in full hearing of a few staff and a lot of lower school students.

So now to face Molly and ask her to be a little more tactful...and quiet!

And so back to exams, English Lit A Level today for which students have to bring in their own texts, which have to be "clean". I resist the chance to tell them that they can't bring in dirty books to the exam – aren't you proud of me?

The fire bell goes off this afternoon – a chemistry lesson has gone awry. An experiment on exploding jelly babies has misfired! This is all discovered after the event.

The fire plan is for students to remain in their seats (the room is a metal and brick box next to the field where the school congregates. Exam papers are to be closed, and students stay in silence whilst I check the situation.

However, best-made plans and all that – the alarm bell is so loud I fear for everyone's ears and sanity, so we have to churn all out onto the field where students are registered and kept away from the rest of the school and from each other as far as possible. In reality, they stand in lines and have invigilators close by to ensure silence. We get priority to return as soon as possible, and time is added on. A form is completed for such an event and returned to the exam board.

Wednesday

Language A Level exams send sound files either via the internet or old style via CDs. One of our students has hearing issues and needs to lip-read. So we have to download a transcript from the exam board website an hour before the exam, give it to a teacher (in this instance, one who can speak Spanish), and then the teacher reads out loud to the student as she lip-reads.

A cumbersome process, but all passes off well. The only thing is that the exam board have already sent out, in paper form with the exam, a transcript – but states that it is not allowed to be opened until the end of the exam! So I have wasted 30 minutes of my time getting online - signing in, getting a code sent to the phone, searching for the file, downloading it, printing it off — when all the time I could just have cut the packet open with my scissors and handed it to the teacher. Think I will be bypassing the process for the next language exams.

The morning session has the biggest GCSE, English Language timetabled with one of the biggest A Levels, Psychology.

Freudian slip – where you say one thing but mean your mother!

Do the people designing the timetable not have any idea about trying to seat over 200 students in a hall, three rooms worth of students on computers, six 1 to 1 students needing readers, scribes etc.

Then some days there are hardly any exams timetabled – think about it, please!

An afternoon phone call from Barney McGrew – can I come and collect a Gary for his Maths exam.

"Why can't he walk here himself – he's a big boy now?"

"Because he hasn't been DBS checked!"

"What?"

"Never mind. I can tell that you are busy, so I will send Dibble down with him."

Turns out that Gary is resitting his Maths A Level, and although a student with us for seven years and well known to all, he left school officially, is now an adult and can't be on the premises without an escort!

I thank Dibble and confirm that I will see him escorted back to Trumpton at the end of the exam.

Gary has a beard these days, well, designer-type stubble, and at the end of the exam, I ask invigilator Niamh to follow him out back to the main office. I point him out to her, so she knows who to shadow.

As I pop out to sort the no-entry boards after the exam, I see Niamh and Gary having a heated discussion in the foyer.

"You need to come with me to the main office?"

"Why?"

"Because you haven't been DBS checked."

"What?"

"We can't let you just walk around the school willy-nilly."

"But I walk all round the school every day...

I feel that I need to interject

"Gary," I start to...

"Who the heck is Gary?

"You are not Gary?"

"No, I'm Phil"

Whoops, the moral of this story – beardy blokes may look the same, but they are not!

Thursday

A student comes to me before the exam

"Sir, I've been sick and had big D all night – don't ask me to spell it out."

"Well, actually, can you because I am writing this book and need to…." I bet Mr Kay knows how to spell it!

"I have had 3 Imodium tablets, so that should plug me up, but just in case I need to run out fast thought I'd better warn you!"

"Thanks for that!"

The student holds fast – or the Imodium does – and makes it through the whole exam without incident

Another stupid clash of the titans with GCSE Science and A Level Biology timetabled at the same time…. WHY?

Today brings the first 3-way clash of the season. Often students have two exams timetabled together.

E.g., Sally has History A Level and French A Level timetabled for a morning session. She can't do both at the same time, so we move one exam (History) to the afternoon and locked her down in between exams.

"Lockdown" was a favourite phrase in the exam world before 2019, so now we struggle to find a better way of describing it.

So this period of "incommunicado" entails the student 'not having access to internet-enabled devices' (the phrase the exam boards like to use).

"Give me your phone and laptop."

This is to ensure that no communication is forthcoming with those having sat the History exam in the morning.

Today we have a 3-way clash for Roger. Unable to do more than 6 hours a day for exams, one has to be held over until the next day. In my first job, I remember students in this category had to go and stay overnight with my Head of Department. Nowadays, such things are fraught with a myriad of potential banana skins, so the perceived wisdom is that a form signed by parents to promise to keep the student away from "internet devices" and to escort them to and from school suffices.

Friday

The analogue clock on the wall has slowly been losing time (despite updating the battery and despite it being radio-controlled). It is now 4 minutes behind. I apologise and mention this to the students. They all look bemused.

"Ok, hands up to those who look at the analogue clock."

They still look bemused

"The round one on the wall with the big hand on 12 and the little hand on 9"

Ah faces now illuminated with recognition

"So, who uses it?"

No hands

"Who uses the digital clock display on the screen?"

Every hand up!

A sign of the times

It's all kicking off. Yesterday's Physics exam has apparently included questions on material not included in the post covid specification.

My inbox is full of irate parental messages, the Head of Physics is asking me what can be done, and students are queueing outside my door.

I tell students to chill, calm the Head of Physics down as she has spent the night in chatrooms, and ignore all the emails. One thing I have learned in this job is that sometimes it is prudent to do nothing.

The whole thing blows over by the end of the weekend when the exam boards admit that they have boobed and assure students that all will be given full marks for that particular question.

And I didn't even break a sweat – result!

I look out across the balcony and see Angie, the invigilator limbering up and doing exercises behind the kids. She has back problems – it reminds me of the Armstrong and Miller Exam sketch where they get involved in a whole host of stuff behind the kids with the admonishment to "face the front" if any try to turn their heads to see what is going on. Check them out on YouTube. And after that plug, can you invite me onto celebrity pointless, please, Mr Armstrong? Although I suppose I could just enter for the "normal" mere mortals programme like everyone else.

In the afternoon, I cause a parent to have a near heart attack. The invigilator taking the register says that John Browne is absent. We double-check his seat, and indeed seat D14 is empty. I rush to Trumpton and get Cuthbert to phone home. Her face grows dark as John's mum says that he left for school an hour ago...in his car!

Now we are all in panic mode as visions of a road collision, ambulances, hospitals etc., fly across our minds. By chance, the Head of Sixth form comes into the office and offers to come back to the exam hall to see if he can spot John. We can't know what every student looks like – but he knows him well.

"There he is, sitting in D15."

AAAAghhhhhh!

Mum is very, very relieved, I feel a bit of a prat, but at the same time, a mixture of relief and frustration - John was sitting in the wrong seat!

Week 6

Monday

Oh Yes, Oh Yes, Oh Yes! Great start to the day! I spot my nemesis, the "Duel" driver, in front of me, the firm's name in massive teasing letters on the back of the lorry. He doesn't see me sneak up, and at the last opportunity, before he has to turn right into the school drive, I put my foot down and without breaking the speed limit (ahem!). I overtake. Yabadabbado! (it reminds me I must tell my Flintstone joke on the next Geography exam.)

People in Dubai don't like the Flintstones

...But people in Abu Dhabi do!

I look in the mirror; can he see my smug eyes? He pretends nonchalance, but I know that he is seething inside. Especially as I slow to a crawl as I head off down the drive, it's a beautiful day!

My happy aura is soon extinguished when I answer the phone to a mum of a student informing me that the student's Auntie had died over the weekend. Turns out that it is the mum's sister and had died quite young. She was very tearful as she was telling me, and it left me feeling all out of sorts. For the poor student, having to get her head down for the next couple of hours isn't going to be easy. Playground duels with lorry drivers are rather insignificant, and next time we meet, I will go over and give him a big hug......Nah!

Back to exam life, I notice that a student is missing from the morning exam. I nip to Trumpton to see if there is any message left with Cuthbert, the attendance officer. I find the whole room in an uproar and the laughing increases in volume as I turn up.

"Just wait 'til you hear this," says Cuthbert.

She plays me the recordings from the absence line.

"Jeremy Smith's dad here, unfortunately, he has a bad throat, possible tonsillitis and will not be able to make the exam today."

She then fasts forward.

"Hi, this is Jeremy Smith's mum, unfortunately, I can't get the lazy g*t out of bed, and so I wash my hands with him. If he fails, then it is down to him..."

Don't they speak to each other? Need to ensure that they are singing from the same hymn sheet. Although perhaps mum is as p***ed off with dad as with son!

Tuesday

Female student in tears outside my office.

"Sir, I know you said don't finish with my boyfriend before exams are over – but he has just finished with me..."

Now to wind back a little to assemblies leading up to the exam period. In these assemblies, I give out lots of instructional stuff but also add in the background stuff like eating well, going to bed at a reasonable time, planning a holiday / excursion / festival for when you finish exams and avoiding making big decisions like "should I be with this person?"

So she has called my bluff because I have no worthy response to being 'chucked.'

I give her a spiel about how it will feel OK in time. She is off to uni soon and won't look back...how I broke up with someone just before my exams, and it turned out well. The trouble is she has an exam in 30 mins, and it ain't gonna heal in that time. Can't help feeling angry with the guy, why now? Just before her final exam.

Probably frustration on his part as she admits that he isn't academic, is working, and doesn't really want her to go away. Oh, the tangled webs we weave.

Jeremy's mum emails me later to ask if there is any chance for a re-sit — possibly, but not until November!

Sometimes we have to let kids fail. It is hard standing by as a parent and watching, but my hope is that in the long term, he will get there. Hard not to be a helicopter parent!

I remember a student I taught as a disaffected 16-year-old at a local FE College. She returned a few years later as a 22 year on an Access course. All fired up and extremely committed, with life and organisational skills honed from working in a shop for a few years, she had set her heart on becoming a nurse ....and she still is one!

"Big bugger up in computer room... get here asap" appears on my smartwatch.

I decided I wanted a smartwatch a couple of years ago and persuaded my wife that it would help immensely at work.

Obviously, I was only 30% convinced of this, and she was only 0.3%. Nevertheless, she bought me one for my birthday.

I have to say that it has become an invaluable tool. We have so many satellite rooms, students on word processors, students needing to be in smaller rooms for anxiety reasons, and students in small 1 to 1 scenarios. So invigilators keep in touch via texting. The watch means that I can look quickly at my wrist and respond accordingly without the need to take my phone out of my pocket.

So I rush to the computer room in response to Meth's "technical" message.

I find Meth and Pete, the invigilator, huddled over a computer with a student sat in tears nearby. Meth ushers me out into the corridor to tell me that the computer has failed and all work has been lost.

Noooooooooooooooooo! The student is 20 mins away from completing the exam when her machine just went blank. I rush to IT whilst Pete calms her down.

No joy from the IT crowd; frustratingly, the autosave has auto failed, and because the student hadn't saved as she went along, it is lost.

"Surely there must be a way to retrieve it?"

"Sadly, No!"

I am so angry...angry with the lukewarm response from the techs, angry with an antiquated system that is just no longer fit for purpose and angry that a student is distraught.

I have to put all these feelings to one side, "park it," as the Head is often saying in line management meetings.

What to do?

    1. Reassure the student that it is not her fault.

    2. Explain that she will need to restart the exam from scratch after a suitable supervised break.

    3. Promise to inform the exam board straight away under their special consideration page.

She responds well, and I take her to speak with her friends in the common room – some of whom have finished the very same exam without incident. It warms my heart to see them grab and hug her and offer messages of support. I have to chaperone her so that no one talks about the exam and then whisk her away to eat and freshen up. Within half an hour, she feels ready to start the exam from scratch. At the end of it all, she looks relaxed and is able to laugh about this incident which will be something to tell her kids and grandkids...ok, let's not get carried away, but after such an awful experience, it was great to see her smile.

I sent details to the exam board straight away, and it is now under their special consideration scrutiny.

Wednesday

The last week of exams and the phone calls keep mounting up.

"Sorry, but Bernard can't make the Maths exam this morning."

"Oh, sorry to hear that. Why not?"

"We're on our way to A and E", Mum shouts over the road noise

Scared that lack of focus may cause more issues and wanting to avoid a major pile-up, I sign off quickly

"Ok, you go and sort and I will chat later."

Invigilator in a satellite room texts to say that "Leah isn't here."

I rush down to Trumpton to check.

Someone once said that two things in life are certain, death and taxes.

In the exam world, two things are certain.

1. A student will misread their timetable and think an exam that is happening this morning is for this afternoon or for tomorrow.

2. One student always breaks a bone – hand, arm, and leg being the top 3.

Leah fits category 1.

We try to find her by ringing home, mum, and dad at work – all to no avail. Eventually, we get hold of grandad, who manages to get a message to her.

Twenty mins later, an Uber rolls up outside, and Leah jumps out wearing shorts and a flimsy top.

"Been on the beach," I ask

"No, ironically, I was at the library revising for this very exam that I thought was happening tomorrow.

We manage to get her into the exam 35 minutes late but still within acceptable limits – full-time is given. I applaud her initiative, no panic, took responsibility, sorted and paid for transport, and handled the drama with a mature philosophical outlook.

Afternoon heralds the GCSE music exam, which I love. It's old-school style on a CD, so we borrow the music department's boogie box and crank up the volume. It always makes me laugh because there are 2 minutes at the start of the exam to read through the paper. Instead of starting the CD after

2 minutes, the 2 minutes of silence are recorded on the CD, i.e., you set the CD running, and 2 minutes of silence actually gets played before the questions kick in.

Thursday

They thought this day would never come! The last GCSE.

I look out across a packed exam hall for the last time this season and wish I had the courage to get them to do a Mexican wave. I have primed an invigilator to record on her phone, so I can release it on youtube, get lots of hits and retire on the proceeds.

But I am too professional and make do with a sad-to-see-you-go and time for one last joke — topically Physics related!

Two brothers have been arrested in Taunton, one for eating batteries, the other for eating fireworks

The Police have

charged one but let the other one off.

My departing shot of "I am here all week" is suffixed with "Happily you won't be" And I encourage them to celebrate but keep an eye out for each other in the hope that all passes off with no dramas.

Drama hits me in the afternoon session. JCQ Inspectors arrive every year to check that we are doing it all properly, and having been primed a few times over the weeks as EOs in neighbouring schools have alerted me with the code words "Elvis has just left the building," I was beginning to believe he was passing me by this year.

So when I answered a call from Dibble, I thought it was a wind-up.

"No, Jim, The Inspector is here."

"Good Joke"

"I wouldn't joke about this"

"Sugar!"

Having only three students in for a Further Maths exam, I had decided at the last minute to house them in a smaller room as the exam hall felt too cavernous. But I hadn't brought over the JCQ bible, 'The Ice Book' (Instructions for Conducting Examinations), which requires a copy in each room.

I run outside the long way around to the exam hall, pick up the ICE booklet and rush it back to the room. I then saunter down to the office to meet and greet Elvis. His name is Percy, and as far from an Elvis lookalike as you can get, he accompanies me round the plot checking off things on his list as we go. I show him the exam hall, the signage, the storage, the exam room being used and the records for students with special exam needs. I get that things have to be checked, and Elvis does it in an efficient but friendly way. As we walk, he asks me about issues with exams, covid, students etc.

I start to mention the AQA issues, and he stops me

"Let me guess."

"Labels" we cry out in unison

Amazing insight from Elvis – well, he is the King!

The AQA label scenario has been bending his ear everywhere he goes. So maybe something will be done.

Not being a toady, but I feel that he is really here to help and advise; yes, he wants to see that things are being done properly, but he isn't about trying to catch you out. I think that I would like to inspect one day, and he is a good role model to follow.

Friday

My wife told me to stop acting like a flamingo
So I've had to put my foot down

And finally – it seemed like it was never going to arrive –but here is the last day of official external exams.

Now you know I said that two things are certain in life, death, and taxes, and that two things are certain in exam life, mixing up dates and breaking bones! Well, having ticked the first box, I was hoping that this was the year I could say that there is an exception to every rule!

Failed!

Open my emails to discover that an A Level student broke her wrist last night and has been kept in the hospital overnight pending an operation this morning. So this morning's Biology paper is going to be one down!

The email doesn't even tell me which wrist has been broken or how it has been broken – is it churlish of me to ask these questions? Obviously, it is all academic if it is the writing hand or not, as this morning's operation has scuppered her chance of sitting the exam anyway. It could possibly be postponed until this afternoon if she can be kept incommunicado – perhaps the doctors can keep her under anaesthetic for a wee bit longer?

So onto my final goodbye pep talk to the students. Unlike the GCSE students who were in on mass for yesterday's final Science GCSE, A Level students, by the nature of their subject choices, have been taking their final exams all week, and so I have been saying goodbye to them in dribs and drabs.

However, with Biology, French, and Computer Science students all in da house, there is a sizeable crowd. In this age group, many drive and even own cars (looking at the road outside, many are newer, swankier, and in better condition than mine). So I urge them to be careful about the drink-drive stuff, urge passengers to think twice about getting into cars, and generally to look out for each other. End of sermon.

On a lighter note, I mention that they can no longer be grumpy around the house at home, that they need to get involved in chores again, and now, if they want to finish relationships...go ahead!

Despite it being the last big exam day, there is still a clash between 2 students. Yes, students study Biology and French – who knew?

So an enjoyable lunchtime with them both under supervision, and then we start the afternoon exam an hour early.

In the morning session, I had to rollock a couple of Year 8 students who found it fun to walk past the no-entry signs singing and kicking a football.

"Cicely Blood is in there doing her Biology exam. She is hoping to go to study medicine at university next year. She needs A* grades to get in.

You two come along making noise, she suddenly loses track of what she is going to write, she struggles and makes mistakes, and she ends up only getting a grade A in Biology.

The uni turns her A* A* A achievements down and deny her entry.

Frustrated, she looks for other courses, but none satisfy her, so she decides to take a year out. Feeling a failure, she sees her friends going away to study – all excited. This compounds her anxiety; she spirals downward, becomes depressed, starts drinking heavily, takes soft drugs, starts stealing from the shop where she works, gets caught, gets arrested, and is given a community service order.

She ends up doing 'community payback' by fixing fences in the local hospital grounds, this makes her even more upset, more drink, harder drugs, gets thrown out of her home, and starts sofa surfing, then friends get fed up, and she is kicked out to live on the streets..."

"What have you get to say for yourselves?"

Suitably chastised faces lift up from staring at their shoes and offer their sincerest apologies

"Sorry, sir, we just didn't think."

"Just didn't think, didn't think, is that going to appease poor Cicely?"

"Can we say sorry to her personally after the exam, sir?"

"Oh, she will be too upset for that; she will be in floods of tears."

"Give us a detention, sir, and then we can write her a letter."

"I'll think about it, but do you know the worst thing of all?"

"No, Sir!"

"You will have deprived the world of the chance to be treated by Dr Blood."

I send them away before I collapse in laughter in the corridor. Meth finds me and asks what is going on, so I relay the tale.

"You can be a real bar steward at times," he concludes.

Meth has an announcement to make to the rest of the team. Something I have known about since before the season commenced. He is stepping down. After 50 years working in education as a teacher, cover supervisor and invigilator, he has decided to walk away whilst he still has some physical and mental abilities to apply to other stuff – just a hunch, but it probably involves more work with trains.

I could not do this job without his help. I inherited him at the start from the previous regime, but as he himself states, the job has become so much more complicated. More and more students with additional needs (word processors, anxiety, scribes, readers, one-to-one attention, etc.) mean that the job has become so far removed from what it once was. Yes, shift happens, but I share his frustration that the infrastructure and staffing have not shifted at the same rate, and the patient is in need of serious resuscitation and aftercare. Whoops slipping into my Adam Kay dream world again. I'm going to miss him.

Big changes are needed for the near future, and whether I will be allowed to see some plans I have in mind being taken seriously will determine if I remain too. Of course, when this book takes off, I will be too busy with bookshop signings, Edinburgh fringe slots, and negotiations for the TV series.

Post Exam Admin Week

A Maths teacher is lying on the floor with blood gushing from her head, a wound caused by a pair of impaled scissors glistening in the sun.

No, not an intro to a new thriller you may think I am trying out (need to do something for a follow-up to book 1), but the result of said Maths teacher saying -

"Ah, great for you; now you can put your feet up for eight months!"

Of course, the vision is solely inside my head but displays the ignorance of some folk to the nature of this job. It's as though they think you just pop up on day one of exams and wing it. A whole year of prep goes into having a successful season.

I won't bore you with the details, but it is like a RORO (Roll On, Roll Off) ferry. One season ends just to herald in the next. I am used to such jibes from people on the outside, but I feel a bit peeved that someone on the 'inside' thinks that way. She will probably say that she was being ironic. Hope so because her mock timetable is going to see Maths placed on the last Friday afternoon.

"Oh well, it's only sums, not like real writing of words and stuff.... So you won't need as long to mark..."

So this week, I am going through all the special consideration requests. Fifty in all so far!

Again the exam boards try and make it as complicated as possible. There is no central place to enter details and send them off; instead, you have to log on to each exam board website (have I mentioned the frustrations with this!). Once in, you have to find the special consideration pages and start entering the details.

There are different sections for students who were absent and those present but adversely affected for some reason. So for each student, I have to go onto four exam boards and put in the same information. Now there is a standardised set of questions, but each exam board sets them out differently – joy!

I have 50 applications so far, so 200 logins and entries to be made

Working through them makes me laugh, almost cry, get angry (with the situation, not the student), and have a whole host of emotions in between.

The JCQ set down basically what you can ask for – and what you can't.

What they say:

Special consideration is given to a candidate who has temporarily experienced illness, injury, or some other event outside of their control at the time of the assessment.

Such things as:

- Temporary illness or accident/injury at the time of the assessment;
- Bereavement at the time of the assessment
- Domestic crisis arising at the time of the assessment;
- Serious disturbance during an examination

And a longer list of what you can't:

- Long-term illness or other difficulties during the course affecting revision time

- bereavement occurring more than six months before the assessment, unless an anniversary has been reached at the time of the assessment or there are ongoing implications such as an inquest or court case;

- domestic inconvenience, such as moving house, lack of facilities, taking holidays

- minor disturbance in the examination room caused by another candidate, such as momentary bad behaviour or a mobile phone ringing;

- the consequences of committing a crime, where formally charged or found guilty; (However, a retrospective application for special consideration may be considered where the charge is later dropped or the candidate is found not guilty.)

- the consequences of taking alcohol or recreational drugs;

- the consequences of disobeying the centre's internal regulations

- quality of teaching, staff shortages, building work or lack of facilities

- misreading the timetable and/or failing to attend at the right time and in the right place;

- misreading the instructions of the question paper and answering the wrong questions

- making personal arrangements such as a wedding or holiday arrangements which conflict with the examination timetable;

- submitting no coursework or non-examination assessment at all

- missing all examinations and internally assessed components/unit
- Exam boards will not give special consideration for something that affects all candidates roughly equally, such as the covid pandemic in general, online teaching during lockdown etc.

Fascinating stuff, the exam boards apply a sliding scale of between 0 and 5% to add to marks depending on how they view the seriousness of the case. The reality is that it is only going to make a difference to students' grades if they are within a couple of marks of a grade boundary.

Exam boards have been fairly secretive about how they apply the SC and usually only tell us that it has been accepted or not. However, over the last couple of non-exam years (but we had assessments remember), schools have had to sort out their own appeal procedures for special consideration - so we have been given more of an insight into how things have been applied.

So wading through the long list highlights the serious stuff some students have to live with. And, of course, this is the tip of the iceberg; many rather keep issues private, some feel it isn't worth bothering about, and some have known no different and accept the abnormal as normal.

So without breaking the confidence and even with changing details wishing to protect students, here are, in general terms, some of the things I am sifting through:

- Death of a parent
- Death of close relative
- Kicked out of home
- Flu/Tonsillitis/Food poisoning
- Surgery
- Car accident
- Parent knocked off bicycle
- Attempted suicide by a parent
- Serious Domestic Crises
- Dog being put down
- Severe panic attacks
- Broken bones

- Computer failure

- Exam paper issues with large print papers having different questions to the smaller print ones.

- Lost cat!

The last one made me laugh out loud, and in sharing with the Trumpton brigade, I asked who felt this was worthy of sending to the exam board.

Most said, "What!" "No way" "Cats are always going off."

Interestingly in a room full of dog obsessives (my judgement), they admit that they would be devastated if their dogs were missing. So is it just pussy prejudice?

Note from my wife: "You can't say that"

But "cat prejudice" doesn't sound as funny!

"Anti-Feline Feeling?"

So I've sent it on to the exam boards voicing my reservation but passing it on up the line so they can sort it. I know I am supposed to filter at this end, but it is a bit of payback, making them jump through a few hoops.

Interestingly not one covid issue throughout the whole exam period. Maybe stop testing, and it goes away?

Mop Up Week

Monday

Although the pressure of the full-on exam season has eased, planning for the next starts to ramp up; already, staff are pinging emails about October mocks, Oxbridge entries (end of September deadline), and Christmas/January mocks. Heads of Department vying for early slots so that marking can be done quickly. RE was the last exam last time, so I intend to put them early in the window.

Pressure always comes from the English department to have early slots because they have 150 students and they write lots, so.... exactly so what! They have five teachers, so tis only 30 students each to mark. History has 90 with three teachers, ergo same ratio, so why can't History take priority? Anyway, various senior management figures in the past have supported the English lobby, so my hands are tied. I do try and rotate all other subjects around so the last (of the year before) shall be first, and so on.

Big John emails me to say that the Head would love to see me to chat about the exam season and future planning. In other words, she wants to get my performance management session out of the way this side of summer.

Tuesday

Meeting with Head

There is an online system where you fill in objectives for the year and then reflect on how they have been achieved or not. Of course, like barristers never asking a question they don't know the answer to, the trick is it set down objectives already achieved or so bland that you can speak in generalisation.

So ones such as:

- *Deliver a successful examination season*

……is so vague that it is easy to give evidence for…

- *Students successfully sat a full range of exams…blah blahdy blah*

Elvis' report has impressed the Head. It is only a set of ticks against a checklist form as they are no longer allowed to make comments like "a well-organised centre" after such a stick was used once to bash the heads of the JCQ after a leaked Maths paper was traced back to a centre where a glowing report had been served.

Despite hardly seeing her during the exam season, she has intriguingly sussed out the experience of students by chatting to them and asking them

"What does it mean to you.,"

Oops, sorry, watching too many Simon Cowell-directed programmes – seriously, Simon asks something different…

So asking them

"How has the exam experience been for you?"

The sly old fox, however, it seems to have paid off in my favour because the "vibe" amongst the students has been overwhelmingly positive. Is this a "down with the kids" approach or an Americanism? Still, she seems happy, and I am happy that she is happy and, more importantly, that the students are happy. My aim is to set a work-like environment where the students know what is what but are wrapped up in a friendly, welcoming atmosphere. Something the Head acknowledges "my team" have managed to pull off. I must pass this on to the "team" when we have our end of exam get together cream tea later this week.

Other objectives from the previous year are ticked off the list or held over for further discussion next year.

With Meth bowing out, I urgently need to think about his replacement, his bed is still warm, but the "king is dead, long live the king" and all that. I had hoped to try and appoint a formal examinations assistant like they have in many schools and to this end have used adverts for such jobs along with their job and personal specifications.

But she is having none of this pleading financial poverty and the seasonal nature of the work. I dispute this seasonal bit as previously mentioned, planning is a year-round event. However, the expected deaf ears make me play my plan B card, which is to use an existing invigilator in a more 'advanced' role without boring you with details to give more paid hours to this person along with training in the ways of the exam business so she can step in if a double-decker bus manages to prevent me dodging it crossing the road.

The problem has been that Meth has given so much time to the role, a lot of it unpaid, that it is impossible to replace like for like. So a whole new dawn awaits!

The failing computer issue has to be sorted – non-negotiable in my eyes, and the Head makes suitable noises in agreement. I have ideas and just hope that they can be in place for the October sessions.

Wednesday

Outside of performance management, I am dealing with requests from exam boards. One student's paper seems to have gone missing. This is more common than you would believe. The exam board have asked me to check that a particular student did sit a particular exam on a particular date. He did!

So now I have to complete their form and send them a register and a seating plan.

I download the PDF form, complete it by hand, scan it back in, and send it back to them. You would think in this day and age. They could send a form I could fill in online and save all this effort!

This is why we keep a record of every student and where they sat in each exam. You never know when you will be called on to show this evidence. I have never been asked to look into a cheating scenario, but it could be useful to see who was sitting next to who if such a case arose.

The exam board have stated that I probably will hear no more from them as they are snowed under! Either the paper will be found somewhere in the system, or a grade will be generated using the other papers sat. In the past, I have been asked to give a ranking of the student relative to the other students in the subject cohort so they can give an appropriate mark. It is a cumbersome process, and the reality of the size of the operation nationally means that mistakes will be made. I know I give the exam boards a bit of stick, but on this issue, I believe they always put the student first.

Thursday

My Twitter feed today tells me that Mr Kay has a new book to be released. I'm not stalking, honest!

Something along the lines of

"For those who have a birthday 15th September, or a Christmas on the 25th December"

Very clever.

I do have his previous book about Christmas season hospital issues, forget the name now. And I have been giving thoughts to my second book after the oh-so-successful feedback on this one! The trouble is a Christmas edition is not really going to generate much interest.

Revising for January mocks – the end!

Anyway, I think I should get in touch with Mr kay and offer to be his support act on his next tour. Surely a 40-minute slot or so would help entertain (but not too much) and warm up the crowd for his big entrance.

Missing Papers:

So far, eight students are deemed to have papers "missing".

As previously mentioned, the first thing the exam boards do is contact and ask if said students were present and can I send the register, the map of where they sat, the date the papers were sent, and the code for the Parcelforce collection.

Now I understand that they want to check that the student was present before they go on a wild goose chase. And I have made mistakes on registers at times. So diligently gather the info, scan, and send. In 2 cases, the students word-processed their work, and I still had their work on our system – so I attached those too.

Only to get a reply to say, "Oh, they have now found the very two word-processed papers." Apparently, they got a little lost in their system as they are taken out from the pack, as they cannot be scanned for marking.

For other 'lost' papers, they advise that they will probably not be in touch again – I suspect that either they will find them eventually – or, as mentioned above - generate a grade based on other papers they have not lost!

Friday

We used to go down to the pub to celebrate the end of the exam season on the Friday after the last exam, but due to a combination of factors – not all invigilators were able to make it, time spent taking down the exam hall, and just generally being absolutely cream crackered we have arranged for everyone to gather round at mine for a cream tea and chance to chill and chat.

So on a beautiful day, it is great to see relaxed, happy smiling faces as scones, cream, jam (debates about the Cornwall or Devon way being the best choice), cold soft drinks, Pimms, and wine are suitably despatched.

At the start of each exam, invigilators are required to be there 20 minutes before (but most come earlier), but the chance for social chat is short-lived as I often have to cut conversations short to get on with stuff needing doing – putting scripts on desks, completing extra time cards, sending some off to satellite rooms with boxes of goodies, etc. So here, as I gaze around, it gladdens my heart to see conversations sparking all over the room.

It is also our chance to say goodbye to Meth, and after a short and witty address by yours truly and present presented, we sit back to hear his speech. Bless him, as he just looks totally bemused, and for someone who has been in education for 50 years, he is lost for words as he bumbles through a response. We let him off the hook as someone gives him a hug, and the emotional temperature ramps up.

"More to eat and drink anyone" saves the day, and folk return to previous conversations. Sitting in the garden after all have gone, Meth admits that he was really choked up and just didn't know what to say. I assure him that his face has said it all...what am I going to do without the old bugger!

Results Week

Cicely Blood is off to be a doctor...much to the relief of the 2 Year 8 boys. Actually, I doubt they will remember anything about it in a couple of weeks when they return as Year 9 boys!

She has ripped open her envelope and whooped across the quad to hug her parents.

It's a great sight, and although some students have asked me to email results out to them, many still want the magic of opening the envelope.

The build-up, the anticipation, the moment they open the envelope, and the joy when they see their grades all add to a real sense of theatre and occasion.

The 'jump in the air' shot, taken about 20 times to get it right for the local press.

As long as it goes well, of course – for some (and it is a small minority this week), things aren't as rosy, and worlds can come tumbling down. This is where the 6th form team earn their money. Sorting out broken dreams and hearts.

Results days are on Thursdays in August. A levels one week, GCSE's the next. However, work begins for the EO early Wednesday morning when the results are ready to download. Via SIMs (the popular school management system), we can download results from the exam boards. It is not always a painless activity, but once downloaded, I have to convert it to meaningful spreadsheets.

Meaningful for the Head, SLT, HODs, and teachers, that is.

How many A*, A, B, etc., or 9,8,7 at GCSE.

Percentages are calculated and set against value-added scores and previous years.

Big interest this year, after two years of no exams (remember we called them assessments, marked them internally, did all the work, and still got charged by the exam boards), to see how it compares with the two fallow years. Compared with 2019, results are looking good.

So note I said that the results are downloaded on Wednesday morning. This means that the chosen few are sworn to secrecy for 24 hours. This has been particularly difficult for me in the past when 2 of my offspring have taken exams at the school – I spent the night in a hotel to make sure that I didn't have to avoid prying questioning eyes from my wife or kids.

So once sorted into a nice colourful spreadsheet, Trumpton folk help me print individual result sheets, head up envelopes and stuff them.

On the morning of the big day, students start to filter in from 08:00. Divided into vague alphabetical cohorts, a steady stream arrives in the first 2 hours.

For A Level students, the majority are moving on to Universities and other higher educational establishments, so sorting their places is the top priority. Those who have achieved their grades for relevant places are fast-tracked through our 6th

Form team and sent happily on their way with congratulations ringing in their ears. For those who have missed by the odd grade, an anxious wait occurs whilst they wait to hear back from their intended next move. Most are still accepted this year, which is good news. A few have been rejected and now need to enter the clearing process to find something suitable, guided by well-equipped school staff.

Some students come to me to ask about re-marks. The exam boards operate a system whereby you can question your exam grades at three main levels.

1. A clerical recheck: This does what it says on the tin and checks that the marks given for the various questions do add up to the total given. Mistakes can be made.

2. Priority Review: This means that your whole paper can be remarked within 15 days. This is mainly for A Level students needing a quick decision for a university place etc.

3. Non-Priority Review: A remark and report which takes around 20 days.

There is a cost which varies across the exam boards, but roughly speaking:

1. Clerical Reviews: £10 - 11
2. Priority Review: £50 - 70
3. Non-Priority Review £40 - 55

This pricing is per paper sat – so most A levels are three papers. A Priority Review for, say, A Level Biology will cost £150 - 170, so not cheap.

The good news is that if your grade changes, you get your money back, whoopee do. But – and 80% of appeals fail – if it doesn't change, you lose!

So students are seeking guidance about whether to stick or twist. I advise them to speak to their teachers, who can look up their actual scores per paper sat. If scores are too far away from the next grade boundary, then it is usually rather pointless. But if very close, the gamble may be worth it. I always advise that, like shares, grades can go down as well as up – so if you have just scraped a grade B, there is a danger that you could lose out and be downgraded.

Three years ago, I got very angry with the system. Kay had applied to a university (I am so tempted to name and shame) and was offered a 3 A* in Sciences to achieve a place on a medics degree. She got:

Physics A*

Chemistry A*

Biology A

The university rejected her straight away.

Now Kay and her teachers were bemused as Biology was by far and away her best subject of the three. Her Biology teacher was so incensed that she paid for a clerical check out of her own pocket. Within a day, the report showed that there had been an error in totting up her marks, and indeed Kay had scored a very high A*

Going back to the university, Kay now presented her 3 A* grades, meeting the offer and expecting that, in good faith, she would now take her well-earned place. Unfortunately, the university had given the place to someone else and were now full. They did offer her a place for the following year! How kind! I have never heard such expletives come from the mouth of a mild-mannered, gentle Biology teacher, but I could only applaud her reaction.

Kay told them to stuff it and went to study that September at a University out East and is really enjoying herself as she continues to train as a doctor.

We received a nice letter from the mum of Sam, who has achieved excellent grades and is off to Oxford to study medicine.

When Sam was 13, we asked what he wanted for Christmas. We were a bit taken back when he asked if he could have some hearts and lungs from the local butcher. Over the next few weeks he began experimenting on devascularisation in the garage. The neighbours were a bit perturbed by the sight of

Sam in a white coat, holding tubes, glass beakers and lumps of offal, with a thin stream of blood trickling out the door into the lane!

Think at 13, I was more interested in eating sweets, playing football, and riding my Raleigh Chopper!

Examination Tips

I realise that since 16, I have been involved in examinations every year, either in doing them myself, teaching and preparing students, being a dad to offspring taking them, and latterly overseeing them as an Examinations Officer.

In reading this book, most of you will have had your own exam experience (good or bad), and many of you will be preparing for your own children taking public exams.

So here are some tips from someone who has seen the process from many angles over many years. There are many books, websites, etc., on how to revise and prepare for exams, and I'm not going to reinvent the wheel and delve headlong into this area but simply offer some hopefully useful ways to navigate through the season.

Tool Up

Gather together the stuff you need to take into an exam.

Get a transparent pencil case (or, failing that put stuff in a clear plastic bag). For obvious reasons, solid pencil cases are not allowed. We can't look at every pencil case to work out that Jennifer, Alison, Phillipa, Sue, Deborah, and Annabel, too, are codes for historical events or biological plants, so sorry, Mr Heaton, your case would be banned.

In the case, have black pens (2 or more). Exam boards ask for black ink these days because they scan your scripts to be marked online; black just shows up best. Pencils, rulers, rubbers, protractors, compasses too and a calculator. My students are told to always bring their calculators. If it is not allowed, just put it on the floor. Other establishments may have different rules about this

– but I feel if your default setting is to put it in your pencil case, then you won't forget it when needed.

RE: drinks – again, the receptacle has to be transparent and should only contain water. I joke with students that I will go around and taste the odd one to ensure no one sneaks neat vodka in. If using a pre-bought plastic bottle, the label has to be removed – yes, a student in another school once wrote helpful hints inside the label.

If you have special dietary requirements and need certain liquids and /or food, arrange all this before the exam season starts. Always, always, put the bottle on the floor, knocked over drinks on desks, and subsequently drying out soggy scripts on radiators is best avoided.

Diet, exercise, and sleep

Not for me to tell you what to eat and drink. But try and eat and drink well. Move about a lot between revision sessions and still partake in your favourite sports and activities as much as you can. Get out in the fresh air more, volunteer to take the dog for walks just make sure that you leave the building. Don't drink a lot of energy drinks.

Work Space

Some are well blessed and have a nice home environment to set up their revision space. Others not so, and if, like me when I was a lad - your home is a little too small or the home environment isn't peaceful - then look at where you can find a space. I used to use what was then the local Polytechnic (now a University) to find a quiet place; public libraries, too, are great for this. Many schools these days set aside places for study and leave students to work during the exam season.

Wherever you are, try and focus on the revision period you have set for yourself. Turn your phone off or leave it elsewhere. You can catch up with your media, social world later.

Although it was this very issue that made it hard to find Leah (see above) when she failed to turn up to an exam, phone calls home and to her mobile didn't help as she had switched off and was ensconced in the local library. Grandad saved the day by finding her.

Playing music can be a help to some – a hindrance to others. As a musician, I know that I can get carried away listening to tunes, so I just can't have music playing. Some can't work without some background. Often a bone of contention between students and parents. Be honest and check that it really is not disrupting you. YouTube has plenty of study-style background music offerings.

Mood Swings

Expect to be grumpy at times. Parents, guardians, and interested parties take particular note of this. It is a stressful time and therefore try to avoid picking up too much on untidy rooms, lack of washing up/chores being completed, monosyllabic conversations, etc. Nothing new to see here - teenage kicks and all that you may think – it just may be more heightened during exams.

Big Decisions

If there are big decisions to be made in your life, leave them until after the exam period. Of course not always possible, but if you are parents/ guardians, now is not the time to mention moving house, or if you are a student in a relationship and are questioning where it is going, now is not the time to end it. I know shift (I don't know if I got the spelling correct there!) happens, so it is not always possible to postpone these things, but where you can – do!

Plan

A revision plan for the weeks before and around the exam is essential. We all work in different ways – I am very much a morning person, rubbish in the afternoons, and useless late at night. You may be the opposite. So plan your revision around your own time clocks.

I used to get up at 5 am, revise till 12 (with breaks), do nothing in the afternoons, do a little more revision early evening, and then stop by 7-8 pm. A friend at uni did not surface from bed until noon worked a bit in the afternoon but did her big shift from 7 pm til 1.00 am

Whatever your clock, plan the slots, build in fun breaks at times, and rotate your subjects around the blocks. Tick off the sessions as you go to give a sense of progression. Put the time and effort in, and it will pay dividends. It is amazing how, in the quiet of the exam hall, when all is focused on the question in hand how, all the information floods into your brain.

By itemising your subjects, you can check what you may have missed if suddenly the dentist offers you a chance to get your filling fixed or long lost cousin Anthony is over from Oz and wants to meet up. You may look back and see that each of these sessions has hit your Biology revision, so you know to focus here and replenish.

Spotting Questions

There has been a bit of a crush leaving an airport in northern Spain.

They have put all their Basques in one exit!

Part of the process of doing exams is trying to work out (guess?) which topics are going to come up – we've all done it. With your teachers, you may be able to work out patterns but beware of putting all of your eggs in one basket:

Don't set your heart on a particular topic appearing. In preparing Sociology students one year, we were sure that Symbolic Interactionism was going to come up on the theory paper – it was due; all other theories had been covered in previous years, and lo and behold, it did come up. Alleluia – er not quite!

Some villains in a shed up at Heathrow (channelling my inner Squeeze here – oh, google it, you young folk!) stole a van full of Sociology and Psychology papers. I'm sure they were hoping for better booty than this but hey-ho! Consequently, new emergency papers were issued, and these did not include questions on Symbolic Interactionism. So beware!

Display Your Timetable

Really look carefully at your timetable, when each exam is, is it a morning or afternoon session, which room you are in and if relevant which seat number.

Display this timetable somewhere prominent in the house (if appropriate) on the fridge/notice board/loo wall! And encourage parents/family to look and help with planning.

If family help is not going to be forthcoming for any reason, share it with a friend so that they will help to remind you. Remember, I have one student every year thinking a morning exam is an afternoon exam.

Plan for Unseen Events

How can I plan for something unseen?

You can't totally, but you can take precautions. If your bus normally just gets you to school just in time, start catching an earlier one during exams. If you get a lift, chat with the chauffeur about leaving earlier. If you are a last minute riser from your bed, train yourself to get up earlier.

Make sure that you have the school phone number in your mobile so that if something happens en route, you can phone ahead and let people know. Don't panic; get there as soon as you can but safely.

Sometimes stuff happens that really has an effect on your performance. Let the Examinations Officer know about this asap, gathering evidence if appropriate. Even with stuff that is very personal, your EO will treat everything in strict confidence.

Cheating

Once upon a time, there was an inflatable boy who went to an inflatable school with inflatable teachers and inflatable students.

One day he took a pin to school and was sent to the Heads office.

"What do you think you're doing?" cried the head

You are going to let yourself down, let me down, let the whole school down!"

Three little words:

DON'T DO IT!

That old saying that "you are only cheating yourself" still rings true.

Chances are you will be caught, and the repercussions are big time. All of your exams will be cancelled - even the ones you haven't cheated in. Parents, friends, and teachers will all feel let down. It is never ever worth the risk.

Fortunately, I have never had anyone cheat in my external exams – although if they have been very good and got away with it, how will I know?

Well, in 2 instances of cheating, I have come across in, mock exams that suggest that I am correct.

In one exam, some males were planning to hide notes in the loo and visit at times to check. Other students got wind of this and shopped them.

In another exam, the student was taking Spanish on a computer. Normally computers have spell check and internet access disabled, but in her case, this had not occurred. The teacher was a little suspicious when this grade 6 student produced grade 9 work – using vocabulary more advanced than he himself would use. The student had gone online and used a high-end translation website!

So usually you will get caught out, if not by your own mishaps, then by other students. Not dobbing/shopping/squealing etc., on others isn't seen as a taboo when it comes to exams. Students want to play fair and will not accept cheating by others.

The main security issue around exams these days is the leaking of papers due to worldwide internet access and differing time zones.

Exam papers are delivered to centres weeks before the exam takes place. And quite rightly, this has been an area of concern for the JCQ inspectorate.

Take my school, where deliveries are made in boxes to the main office. Here one of the Trumpton crew signs for it and contacts me straight away.

I then go to collect the boxes and take them to my double-skinned triple-locked safe room, where I sort out from the boxes onto shelves according to the timetable. I sign these in and check against the inventory lists sent.

Exams are in sealed plastic envelopes and can only be opened an hour before each exam takes place. They have to be opened in the presence of "2 pairs of eyes". Usually, Meth and I open and sign to say that they were sealed until we took the big scissors to them.

Students often ask me how much they can pay me to let them see the paper before the exam.

What do you think...£1 million sounds about right?

Look Out For Each Other

Exams bring stress, no way of avoiding it. It is a normal state of affairs. Having said that, for some students, levels of anxiety are way above what could be considered as 'normal par for the course'.

Never suffer in silence – speak to someone about this; a friend, family member, teacher, counsellor, or doctor.

Look out for each other, and keep an eye on your friendship circles. Some things are beyond your remit, so don't get bogged down in helping when you recognise things are more serious – just let someone know – teacher, exams officer, etc.

Plan Nice Things Post Exams

Weirdly finishing exams can feel a bit like a bereavement! You look forward to them being over, but the process has kept you occupied, and now you may not know what to do with yourself.

For A Level students particularly (and some leaving GCSE students), this marks the end of your school life, and suddenly the future looks a little uncertain. Again this is all very normal, and all will be well, but it can be a little discombobulating!

Before exams, plan to do something, go to a festival, go on holiday (chance to take cheap bookings before schools are out for the summer), visit friends, go for lots of walks, spend a day shopping...whatever fits your interests and budget. But do something!

Keep Perspective

As I write the wonderful song by Travis and gorgeous Susanna Hoff (indulge this old man and his younger Bangle loving days)

When I held you, it was the only thing
Only thing
And all I knew was you were everything
Everything

https://www.youtube.com/watch?v=0OL2zAQM
Nak

It's not!

Ok, so he is talking about a relationship but taking up the "the metaphor, the metaphor" it might have felt like it for a few weeks, but it is not the only thing!

Yes, they can be important rites de passage in life, but they are not the most important things.

Enjoy your exams but keep them in their place.

Remember:

THEY ARE ONLY EXAMS

Acknowledgements

Thanks to some amazing invigilators who have gone beyond the call of duty and made my working life so much easier. A special bottom of my heart thanks to Meth – my wife read the intro to this book and said..." I hope you are going to say some nice things about Meth."

So to keep her off my back.... seriously, he has been my wingman throughout my tenure in this job, and heaven knows how I will replace him now that he has decided to hang up his -well, whatever chief invigilators hang up. It is fair to say I could not do this job without his assistance. He has put in far more hours than he has ever claimed for and always goes the extra mile. He has been in the front line when I have lashed out, been the sponge to absorb my frustrations and whatever the hour. Early dawn or late finishes after school ...is always there to ensure the smoothest running of exams.

Since I stopped teaching and took up this role, I have had the privilege of walking around the school time after time and enjoying peering into classrooms and watching these talented people go about their craft – some seriously good stuff is going on in classrooms!

And to the hundreds of students I have seen come through the exam hall in the last few years...some great kids...apart from the Year 12 idiot who thought it was fun to continually disturb those in the exam hall by kicking a ball against it and running away – I hope that you fail all of your exams!

Glossary

A Levels – National exams taken at 18 in England and Wales

Adam Kay – Ex medical doctor and author

AQA/Edexcel/OCR/WJEC – The 4 major exam boards producing subject exams

CAMHS – Children and Adolescent Mental health Services - helps young people suffering with mental health issues

D Of E – Duke of Edinburgh - an award system devised by the late Duke of Edinburgh to encourage young people's participation in challenging events

DBS – Disclosure and Barring Service - a national register to ensure that people working with children and youths are suitably vetted

Edinburgh Fringe – Famous Arts festival based in Scotland's capital

EO – Examination Officer

GCSE – General Certificate of Education - National exams taken in England and Wales at the age of 16

Half Term – UK schools usually divided into 3 terms of 12 - 14 weeks. Half term is a week long holiday in the middle of the term

Haribo – Sweets/Candy

Head – Head Teacher - Principal

HOY – Head of Year - Schools in England and wales are divided into Year groups based on age cohorts

ICE – Instructions for Conducting Examinations - reference book for all schools/colleges to follow the same national guidelines

Invigilator – Person who polices exams to monitor the process

JCQ – Joint Council of Qualifications - the body responsible for monitoring exams in England and Wales

JCQ Inspector – Visiting external inspector to ensure that all schools/colleges conform to the same standards for exams

They visit annually and file a report

Loo – Toilet/Bathroom

M1 M5 etc. – Names for main motorways (freeways) in UK

Mocks – Test exams - students take as trials before the 'real' exams

Monty Python – 1970s UK popular comedy series

Oz – Australia

Parcelforce – UK based collection and delivery service

Pimms – English alcoholic drink - a gin based fruit cup popular in summer

Raleigh Chopper – Bicycles popular in the 1970s - a small front wheel and large back wheel

Richard Osman – TV presenter and author

Robin Hood – Legendary English outlaw/freedom fighter

SLT – Senior Leadership Team - The Head (Principal) and Deputy Heads/Assistant Heads

Sodor – Island where a children's programme about steam trains is based

Squeeze – British band

The Beano – UK Comic book

Uncle Bryn – Welsh character in popular UK comedy programme - Gavin and Stacey

Watch With Mother – 1960s young children series